**BROOKE CARTER**

ILLUSTRATED BY

**ALYSSA WATERBURY**

ORCA BOOK PUBLISHERS

Published in Canada and the United States in 2023 by Orca Book Publishers.
orcabook.com



**Library and Archives Canada Cataloguing in Publication**
Title: Ghost girl / Brooke Carter ; illustrated by Alyssa Waterbury.
Names: Carter, Brooke, 1977- author. | Waterbury, Alyssa, illustrator.
Series: Orca echoes.
Description: Series statement: Orca echoes
Identifiers: Canadiana (print) 20220477167 | Canadiana (ebook) 20220477205 | ISBN 9781459836884 (softcover) | ISBN 9781459836891 (PDF) | ISBN 9781459836907 (EPUB)
Classification: LCC PS8605.A77776 G56 2023 | DDC jC813/.6—dc23

Library of Congress Control Number: 2022950486

**Summary:** In this partially illustrated early chapter book, ten-year-old nonbinary Sly works to solve riddles and locate the spell that can save them, their grandmother and a ghost girl from being stuck forever in an enchanted mirror.

Orca Book Publishers is committed to reducing the consumption of nonrenewable resources in the production of our books. We make every effort to use materials that support a sustainable future.

Orca Book Publishers gratefully acknowledges the support for its publishing programs provided by the following agencies: the Government of Canada, the Canada Council for the Arts and the Province of British Columbia through the BC Arts Council and the Book Publishing Tax Credit.

Cover artwork and interior illustrations by Alyssa Waterbury
Edited by Debbie Rogosin

Printed and bound in Canada.

26 25 24 23 • 1 2 3 4

FOR PAULINE,
WHO LOVED
EVERYTHING ABOUT
HER GRANDCHILDREN.

I don't get scared easily. I love horror stories and scary places. Even the tales about Madsen Mansion—my grandma's mysterious old house—didn't bother me. I couldn't wait to stay for a whole weekend. It was the only good thing about moving across the country. But when Mom and I pulled up to the mansion on Friday night, I got chills. Now I understood where the nickname "Madness Mansion" came from. The place gave me the creeps!

The sun was setting behind the house, leaving the front in darkness and casting an eerie orange glow over the grounds. A low mist floated across the driveway. Deep shadows stretched between the trees. As the bare branches scraped together in the wind, they seemed to come alive. I shuddered and looked away just as a flurry of black wings swooped down over the rooftop. Bats! It was like a scene from a movie. My heart pounded with excitement.

I'd never visited Madsen Mansion before. Sure, I'd seen Grandma Madsen lots of times when she'd visited us, but this was the first time I'd ever been to the place where my mom grew up. I wished it was a visit just for fun and not because I needed somewhere to stay while my mom set up our new place. Our new place across the country from Dad, away from our old life together, our family split in two.

The mansion looked as scary as I'd imagined. It had a pointy tower on one side and lifelike statues of wolves along the roof. Iron bars protected the large windows, and the heavy double doors seemed like the gates to a castle. There was no way someone could break into—or out of—those doors. Mom said the house used to be a sunny yellow, but now the paint was dirty and peeling. If you googled "haunted house," this is what you'd see. But it couldn't really be haunted, could it?

Mom parked at the top of the circular driveway. "Here we are, Sly. Your home for the weekend. What do you think, honey?" She looked at me with a twinkle in her eye.

I shrugged. "I've seen scarier," I said. That was a fib.

Mom smiled. "I'm going to miss you." She reached out to stroke my face. I could see her eyes welling with tears. *Oh no.*

"Mom, stop it! I'm ten." I swatted her hand away. "I'll see you on Sunday morning."

"It has been too long since I was here," Mom said as she looked up at the house. "I used to sleep in the tower."

I followed her gaze to a half-open window waiting in darkness. "Sometimes I thought I could hear someone calling my name."

I shivered. "Nice try, Mom."

"What?"

"You're just trying to scare me."

She smiled. "Am I?"

Just then I saw something move in the tower window. I hoped it was only the curtains flapping.

"Mom, is there anything else I should know about this house?" I asked.

Mom laughed. "Believe me, it was interesting growing up here with your grandma. It's a...special place."

I smiled. "Okay."

As we walked up the cobblestone path, the rosebushes reached out to scratch us as we went by. There were symbols carved into the wide doors. They looked like stars and letters, but I couldn't read the fancy writing.

"What is that, Mom?" I asked.

"Gaelic," she said. "An old language. The language of our ancestors."

"What does it say?"

"It's hard to explain," she said. "It means that this door is the threshold between without and within."

"Huh?"

Mom laughed. "Exactly. You'll find that this place is full of mysteries."

"Cool," I said, but a shiver ran through me all the same. "Should we knock?"

"I'm sure she already knows we're here," said Mom. And with that the big doors groaned open, spilling warm light at our feet. I jumped as a dark shadow appeared in the doorway.

"My vision," said the shadow, "has come true."

The doors swung inward, and the shadow stepped out. It was Lady Madsen, fortune teller and local legend. Also known as Grandma.

"Hi, Grandma," I said, feeling a bit shy.

Lady Madsen was no ordinary grandma. She wore a flowy dressing gown with stars and moons and mysterious symbols on it. Her hair was big and white and wiry. Her eyes twinkled.

She must know lots of juicy secrets, I thought.

"Sly," said Grandma. "Heart of my heart." She seemed to float toward me in her robe.

"Thank you for inviting me to stay with you," I said, remembering my manners. "I've always wanted to see Madness—

I mean, Madsen—Mansion." I grimaced. *Oops.*

But Grandma laughed. "I've always loved that name. Madness Mansion! How wonderful." She opened her arms and gathered me in for a tight hug. She smelled like cookies and fancy candles.

"I'm so happy you're here, Sly, and at the very best time of year."

"Oh, because it's Halloween?" I asked. "I'm not into trick-or-treating anymore, so don't worry."

"Halloween? Humph, no." Grandma shook her head, and her hair waved at me. "I mean Samhain, the most important night of the year."

She whispered, "It's when the spirits can cross over into our world. And it's tomorrow."

Grandma was sweet even if she was weird. Weird I could handle. I was kind of weird too. But spirits? Was Grandma trying to scare me?

Mom cleared her throat. “I’ve got to go. Lots to do getting things moved in this weekend. I want everything settled by the time Sly starts their new school next week.”

*Ugh*. New school. As if I didn’t have enough to worry about with Mom and Dad splitting up. I don’t like new things.

“Hmm,” said Grandma as she looked at me. “Yes, lots of new things for Sly.”

*Wait. Did she just read my mind?*

“It’s too bad you can’t stay,” Grandma said as she hugged Mom. “But thank you for bringing my sweet grandchild.”

“Are you ready, Sly?” Mom asked.

I nodded, but I wasn't ready. Not yet. I wasn't ready to stay alone in this big scary place. I wasn't ready to hang out with a grandma who I was pretty sure had some kind of magical powers. I wasn't ready for Mom to go yet. I wasn't ready for her to move us into our new place. And I wasn't ready for being in two families instead of one. I needed two of me, it seemed, but I was one person. Just Sly, pulled in two.

Mom gave me a hug, holding on longer than usual. I knew she was nervous too.

"Sly has everything they need," she said to Grandma. "They're ten now, so they're all grown up."

Grandma winked at me. "I see that. They certainly are bigger than the last time I saw them."

"Call me later," Mom said.

"Maybe not," said Grandma with a cheeky smile. "We're going to be busy having fun. Come on in, Sly, if you dare." She stepped aside and motioned to the open door.

I wished Dad was here. Ever since Mom and Dad had decided to live apart, it was like Dad was fading away. He was kind of like a ghost now, I thought.

I shivered and pulled my long black cape around me. It was my favorite item of clothing. It was soft and had a pointy collar and a hood.

Mom had made it for me a couple years earlier, when I was a vampire for Halloween, but now I wore it all the time. That started around the time I changed my name to Sly. The cape suited me. It fit me like my new name did—and my new haircut. Mom had shaved one side of my hair short, and the other side fell in a swoop over my right eye. I liked soft clothes that didn't dig in, and I hated anything tight around my tummy. So I liked to wear my dad's big button-down shirts over leggings, with my cape and a pair of boots. Like this, I was the most "me" I'd ever been.

"This house is a special place. A thin place," said Grandma.

"A what?" I asked.

"A place where the veil between worlds is thin and the spirits can squeeze through," she said. "Come in and see the house. It has been waiting for you."

Goose bumps popped up all over my body. I pulled my cape even tighter and stepped across the threshold.

Grandma shut the heavy doors behind me. The sound echoed, and it was no wonder—this place was huge!

"Wow," I whispered. Madsen Mansion was as cool as I had imagined. The entrance opened into a massive room with a high domed ceiling covered in swirling designs. The room was round and lit with a sparkly chandelier. A giant staircase curved up the wall to the right. Old paintings dotted the walls—picture after picture of people dressed in old-fashioned clothing on the grounds of Madsen Mansion. Were these my ancestors?

"This is the great room," said Grandma. "But I like to think of it as the family room, because it has generations of Madsens watching over us."

I felt a chill. "Um, Grandma, don't you feel a little creeped out with all those eyeballs following you?" I nodded to the paintings. Dozens of eyes seemed to watch us as we walked.

"Not at all." Grandma laughed. "I always keep this room open, along with the tower room, my bedroom, my reading room and the kitchen, of course. Everything else is closed."

"Closed?" I asked. I was still trying to take it all in.

"Off-limits," said Grandma. "There is no staff here, Sly, and it's a big place. I can't keep it up by myself."

"Do you ever think about moving?" I asked.

Grandma stopped walking and looked deep into my eyes. "Never. I keep this home because it is special to our family. I will always be here."

"But aren't you lonely?"

Grandma smiled. "Oh no, sweetheart. I have friends. And the townsfolk come to have their fortunes read. Besides, you're here now, and we're going to have a great Samhain."

A bell sounded from a grandfather clock. *Bong!* I counted six slow tones.

"Ah," said Grandma. "Six o'clock. Time to eat, yes?"

My tummy rumbled. "Yes, please," I said. I was suddenly very hungry.

Grandma took my hand, and we walked down a narrow hall to the kitchen. It looked like something out of a restaurant. There were three ovens, a walk-in fridge and a huge sink that looked big enough to swim in. The floor was made up of black-and-white checkerboard tiles.

"Apple pie and ice cream for dinner?" asked Grandma.

"Um, sure," I said in disbelief. I could hear Mom's voice in my mind. *Sugar, sugar, sugar.*

"A little sweet is good for the soul," said Grandma as she set our dishes on the counter and loaded them up.

I looked around for a table.

"Where do we eat?" I asked.

"There is a formal dining room upstairs," said Grandma, "but it's closed, and the furniture is covered in sheets. Besides, it's too big for two people. I like to eat here. Pull a stool up to the counter."

"Okay." That was fine by me. I used to eat at the counter in my old house. Would I do it in my new house?

As we ate, Grandma reached out and touched my cape. "Tell me about this," she said.

I put my spoon down. "I don't know," I said. "It makes me feel...like me. Safe. I don't know how else to say it."

Grandma nodded. "I understand," she said. "I like your cape. And I like your hair too. In fact, I like everything about you."

She winked, and I couldn't help but wink back.

"We'll have to leave some pie for the spirits," she said.

"The what?"

"It's a Samhain tradition," she said. "We leave food for the hungry spirits who cross over."

"Hungry spirits?" I asked. "Hungry for food, right? Not for people?"

Grandma laughed. "You watch too many scary movies. The spirits are harmless. Unless..." She trailed off.

I gulped a bite of pie. "Unless?"

Grandma leaned in. "Unless they lure you to the Otherworld. So be wise to any strange mists, and don't go stepping into fairy rings."

Now it was my turn to laugh. "Okay, Grandma," I said. "I won't."

I scooped up the rest of my pie and immediately bit into something hard.

"Blech," I said as I spat it out. It was a little stone charm with a symbol on it that looked like a knot. "What is that?"

"Ah!" said Grandma with delight. "You found the Samhain prize! It's a tradition. The prize is hidden in a cake or pie, and whoever finds it is blessed."

"What does it mean?" I asked. I didn't say how weird I thought it was to put rocks in people's pie.

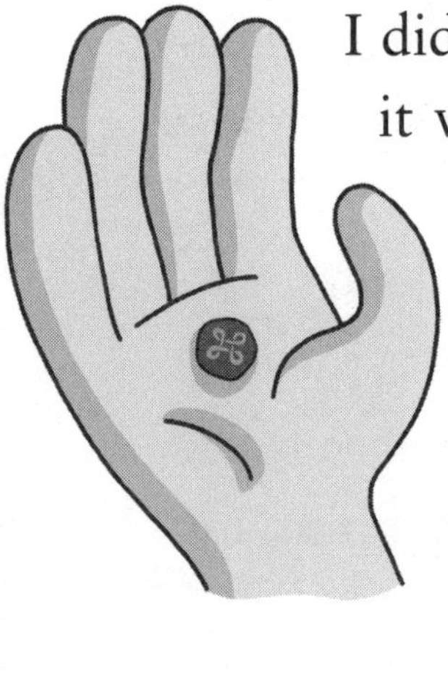

"That's a Bowen knot," Grandma said. "It's a symbol of protection."

"Can I keep it?" I asked.

"Of course."

Grandma handed me the half-empty pie dish. "This is for the spirits. Put it on the doorstep."

She opened the kitchen door, and crisp fall air rushed in.

It was very dark. I placed the dish on the cracked stone steps and looked out across the grounds. Was that a cemetery in the distance?

As I hurried back into the kitchen, I noticed a funny little sliding door in the wall, with some buttons beside it. "Hey, what is that?"

"Oh, that's a dumbwaiter."

"A what? That's not a very nice name," I said.

"No, I suppose not," Grandma said. "It's like a little elevator. The kitchen staff used it to move things between floors so they didn't have to carry heavy trays."

"Neat." I took a closer look.

"I'll tell you a secret," said Grandma. She slid the door open. "When your mother was young, she would hide in here. And sometimes she would even ride from floor to floor." She narrowed her eyes at me in a challenge. "Are you brave enough to try it?"

My heart thumped with excitement. "Yes!"

"Then climb in," said Grandma.

I got inside. There was just enough room for me to sit cross-legged.

"I'll slide the door shut," said Grandma, "and press the button to move you up. There's a little rope pulley inside that you can use to come down. Just tug on it. Okay?"

"Got it," I said.

Grandma closed the door, and as soon as she did, I wished I hadn't gotten in.

It was so dark inside. But then the little elevator started to move. Up, up, up. It went slowly, and I wondered how long it would take to get to the top. And where would I end up?

When the elevator stopped, I slid the door open and peeked out. There was a long, dark hallway filled with mirrors. Big mirrors, round mirrors, tall mirrors, square mirrors—every shape and size you could imagine. But something about that hallway scared me. I couldn't explain it.

I slid the door shut and was just about to pull the rope to go back down when I heard a faint voice. I opened the door again. There was no one there—just endless mirrors. *Weird*. I shivered.

I shut the door quickly and pulled the rope. Nothing happened. I pulled again. Nothing.

*Sly*.

Someone had just said my name. Or was it just in my head?

"Who's there?" I whispered.

Silence.

I gave a desperate tug on the rope, and the dumbwaiter lurched. *Finally!* I wanted to get away from that hallway. I thought about what Mom had said—how she used to hear someone calling her name. I decided it was probably just a trick she and Grandma were playing on me.

The dumbwaiter stopped one more time, opening onto a dusty old room with furniture covered in white cloths. This must be the dining room. Nothing scary here. No voices. I shut the door and pulled the rope, and then I was back in the kitchen with Grandma.

"Nice ride?" she asked.

"You could say that," I said. "But that mirror hallway is super creepy. And I don't really like having tricks played on me."

Grandma frowned. "Mirror hallway? This elevator only goes to the dining room. There is no mirror hallway. And what are these tricks you're talking about?"

"Nice try," I said. "Were you trying to scare me by saying my name in an eerie voice?"

"No. I wouldn't do that to you," said Grandma, and as soon as she said it, I knew it was true.

"I guess I must have been hearing things then."

We stared at each other in silence.

"But I still don't understand about the mirror hallway. That was real. It had to be."

Grandma put her warm hands on my shoulders, and it calmed me down. "Well, this is an old house," she said. "A house with secrets that even I don't know about. It has a life of its own. And perhaps this mirror hallway you speak of is..."

"What?" I asked. "Is what?"

"A mystery," she said, and shrugged.

I nodded. But those mirrors were stuck in my mind.

"Why don't I show you my reading room?" Grandma asked.

"Okay," I said, grateful to think about something anything—else. "I do love books. Got any graphic novels?"

"No, silly. Not that kind of reading," she said. "I'm going to read your fortune."

Things were getting weirder by the minute.

Grandma's reading room was not what I'd expected. I'd thought it would look like a library, but it was much more than that. The room was round, and it seemed like there were circles everywhere. A round red rug. A round wooden table. A big round window like a ship's porthole. Even the picture frames were round, and they were filled with old photographs of Madsens from the past.

But the best round thing in the room was a pink crystal ball in the center of the table. It was shiny and gave off a warm glow. I wanted to touch it.

"It calls to you, doesn't it?" We sat across from each other, and I stared at the crystal ball. It had swirly stuff inside it that seemed to move. Was it real? Or was it just a prop like the ones in my favorite horror movies? I'd seen enough behind-the-scenes specials to know that it could be a trick of the light. Maybe there was a hidden switch somewhere?

"I've had this crystal ball since I was a little girl," Grandma said. "I got it from my aunt, who got it from her aunt, and so on and so on. Many generations of Madsens have used it to read fortunes. Maybe you will too one day."

*Me?* A thrill ran through my body. "Cool," I said. I looked at the faces on the wall. Was I like them?

One of the pictures caught my eye. It was of a girl around my age, but she looked sad. Suddenly the hair on my arms stood up.

"Weird," I said.

"What is it?" asked Grandma.

I pointed to the painting. "That girl. Who is she?"

"Ah," said Grandma. "That would be a distant cousin from long ago. A very sad story."

"Tell me," I urged.

"Her name was Maeve. She was very sick. Her mother, Mildred Madsen, was a powerful witch."

"A witch?"

"Of course!" said Grandma. "All Madsens are witches." She shrugged like it was no big deal.

"Anyway"—Grandma leaned forward—"Mildred was working on a spell to open a door to the in-between. She wanted to find a way to keep Maeve alive. But before Mildred could complete the spell, Maeve disappeared. It was Samhain. And she was never seen again."

"What happened to the witch? I mean, Mildred?" I asked.

"She died of grief."

"That's so sad."

"Yes," said Grandma. "Over the years people have said they could hear a voice calling from the tower, where Maeve was last seen."

I gulped.

Grandma lit some candles and then reached for my hands.

"Don't be afraid, Sly," she said.

"I'm not afraid of anything," I said. Before today that was true. But Madness Mansion was doing its best to test me.

Grandma smiled. "Then you can handle whatever comes your way." She winked at me again, and I decided I liked the way the skin around her eyes crinkled up. She must have spent a lot of years winking at people. I hoped I would get lines like that one day. Happy winking lines.

Grandma closed her eyes and concentrated. She made some little humming noises, and when she opened her eyes, she looked deep into the crystal ball.

"Oh yes," said Grandma. "A vision. You will live a long and happy life."

She could see the future?

But before I could ask her, Grandma frowned. "Unless..." She trailed off.

"Unless?" I asked. "Unless what?"

Grandma shook her head. "It's not clear. There's a mist in the way. Something I cannot see. Something that is not of our world."

"What does that mean?" I asked. Okay, I was definitely getting freaked out.

"The in-between," said Grandma.

"What's that?" I asked.

"I see you stuck between two places," she said. She raised a penciled eyebrow at me.

I sighed. “Yeah. That’s me. Always in between things,” I said.

“The best people are mysteries, Sly,” said Grandma. “Being an in-between person is a gift.”

I nodded.

“Now would you like to make a wish?” asked Grandma. “It’s Samhain tomorrow. The spirits are listening.”

A wish? But what could I ask for?

"Anything," said Grandma, as if I had spoken out loud. "Place your hands on the ball."

I put my hands on the cold crystal and closed my eyes.

"Make your wish, Sly," Grandma said. Her voice seemed far away.

"I wish," I said. "I wish that I will always know the right thing to do."

I opened my eyes.

Grandma smiled at me. "What a wonderful wish."

The old clock in the great hall began to chime. I counted nine bells.

"Nine o'clock already? But how is that possible?" I asked.

"Time is different in this house," said Grandma.

What does that mean? I wondered.

"Time for bed," said Grandma. "You will be sleeping in the tower."

The tower? After all that she had told me?

"Come," she said. "It's quite a beautiful room. You'll see."

I followed her to the great room and grabbed my backpack.

She led me up the curved staircase to a small doorway that opened to another stairwell. This one was narrow and winding. We climbed and climbed.

Finally we reached a small hallway with two doors. One had a carved *M* on it. *M* for Madsen? I wondered.

Grandma opened the door, and I gasped.

Inside was the coolest bedroom I had ever seen. It was a hexagon! It had fancy old wooden furniture and a four-poster bed with curtains. There were stained-glass windows, and the light from the table lamps made them glow and fill the whole room with rainbow light.

"Awesome!" I said. I was still a little nervous because of Grandma's story, but the amazing room made up for it.

"I will leave you to unpack and get to bed," said Grandma. "There's a little bathroom across the hall. I'm going to get started on a special breakfast for tomorrow. Waffles! And the batter needs to rest."

"I love waffles!"

"I know," said Grandma.

"Did you read my mind?" I asked.

"No, I asked your mom."

We both laughed.

"If you need anything, just use the speaking tubes."

"The what?" I looked around. What was she talking about?

Grandma walked over to a small hole in the wall, circled by a brass ring. She leaned in close and whispered something into it. Her voice came from behind me. "Hi, Sly."

I spun around. There was another, smaller hole where her voice came out.

"Neat!" I said.

"Wherever you are in the house, I can hear you if you talk into one of these tubes. They're all connected inside the walls."

"Okay." I couldn't wait to try them out.

Grandma gave me a warm hug. "Good night, my dear."

"Good night, Grandma," I said. "I can't wait for Samhain!"

Grandma winked at me again. "Nothing is ever lost as time passes," she said. With that she left, her robes twirling. The clock on my bedside table said *9:30*. I yawned.

I pulled my dinosaur-print pajamas from my backpack and got changed. Then I pulled my cape on over top. I put the rest of my stuff in the dresser near the window.

All the old furniture in the room was polished and gleaming, but there was one large item covered with a sheet. It was as if it had been forgotten there. I didn't think I could sleep with it covered up like that, so I pulled off the sheet.

Underneath was a very old cabinet with double doors held closed by a heavy metal lock. Both doors had the letter *M* carved on them, along with the same symbol I'd

found in the pie. What was that called? A Bowen knot, Grandma had said.

I ran my hand along the symbol, and a cold feeling rushed up my arm. I backed away, then turned and ran to the bed, pulling the curtains closed.

I fell asleep, the mysterious knot symbol floating in my mind.

*Sly*. A voice was calling to me. *I need your help, Sly*.

I opened my eyes, groggy from a fitful sleep. All night I had had strange dreams about the cabinet and about voices calling my name.

"Sly." Grandma's voice came from the speaking tube. "Waffles are ready."

"Yes!" I hopped out of bed, hurried through the door and raced down the staircase to the kitchen, my cape flying behind me.

“Happy Samhain!” said Grandma. She had made a huge spread of waffles, with all kinds of toppings.

For a little while I forgot all about the strange events from the night before as we tucked into breakfast.

“What are we doing today?” I asked once I was finished.

"I thought we'd go into town to get apple cider, do some shopping and then come back and build a bonfire."

"Yes!" I said. "Can we roast marshmallows?"

"You bet," said Grandma. "Now go get some warm clothes on and meet me down here."

I went back to my room, a little slower now that I was weighed down by Grandma's waffles.

I was grabbing my leggings when I heard someone say my name, and this time it was not just in my head.

"Sly."

I whirled around. "Who's there?" My heart thumped. The voice wasn't coming from the speaking tube. It wasn't Grandma.

"Sly," the voice said again, and I realized it was coming from the mysterious cabinet.

Then again, louder this time.

"Sly, help me."

The voice sounded sad, and I knew it was the same voice I had heard in the mirror hallway.

"I'm trapped."

On wobbling legs, I crossed over and gave the doors a tug, but the cabinet wouldn't open. There was no keyhole in the lock, and I realized that it must be a puzzle lock. Dad had told me all about them and had even shown me some videos of people solving them.

I fiddled with it, and the center of the lock twisted to the left. But it didn't open. I pushed on a star-shaped part in the middle, and a skinny piece the size of a hairpin popped out. What was I supposed to do with it? I looked at the lock and saw a little groove on the back where the skinny piece might fit. I pushed it in, and the lock suddenly sprang open. I had done it!

With shaking hands, I opened the cabinet doors. To my disappointment, there was no one inside. Nothing scary at all. But wait! There at the very back of the cabinet, right at the bottom, was the Bowen-knot symbol, carved into the wood.

"Weird," I said. I ran a finger across it, and a secret door creaked open a bit.

I pulled the door open all the way to see...me!

"A mirror," I whispered. But why would anyone want to hide a mirror?

As I stared at my reflection, strange letters floated across the mirror. It looked like the Gaelic words that were on the front doors of Madsen Mansion.

I couldn't understand what they meant, but I sounded them out.

"Doras fosgailte."

And then the second line. "Beatha ùr."

The words disappeared and then I saw something shimmer. A white figure appeared right beside me. It was floating! It was a ghost!

I screamed and ran to the bed, pulling the curtains closed.

"Grandma," I whispered into the speaking tube beside the bed. "Grandma, there's a ghost."

But there was no answer. All I could hear was my own pounding heart.

"Hello?" said a faint voice. "Please come back."

I pulled open the curtains.

Staring back at me from the mirror was a girl. A ghost girl. She had a sad face and long dark hair. She wore a white nightgown.

"What is happening?" I asked.

"You can see me!"

"You're a ghost. Ghosts aren't real." I leapt from the bed and ran for the door.

"Wait! Please don't go," called the girl. "I'm stuck. And it has been such a long, long time since anyone has been able to see me."

Looking at our faces next to each other in the mirror, I recognized her. "You're Maeve. The girl from the painting."

"Yes."

"Wow!" I exclaimed. "I'm Sly. Sly Madsen. I think we're cousins."

"I know," said Maeve. "I can see and hear everything in this house, but no one can see me. Until now."

She must have been the one calling to my mom all those years ago. I felt terrible for Maeve. She must have been so scared and lonely.

"But how can I get you out?" I asked.

"This mirror is enchanted," she said. "I've been waiting for someone to complete the spell."

I felt dizzy. Enchanted? Complete the spell? And could I, *should* I, set her free? I imagined being stuck somewhere for years and years. I would want someone to help me too. And this ghost girl, Maeve, well, she didn't seem that scary.

"I will help you," I said, and as soon as I did, I knew it was the right decision. "Just tell me what to do."

"It's Samhain," she said. "It's the only time of year the spell can be completed. But I can't do it myself."

"Tell me how," I said.

"There is a missing part of the spell. Someone from the living world must speak the rest of it."

"The rest of it?" I said.

"Yes," said Maeve. "You spoke the first two lines. 'Doras fosgailte. Beatha ùr.' It means 'An open door. A new life.'"

"I said a spell?" I asked in disbelief.

Maeve nodded. "And only someone with the gift can do that."

The gift? Maybe I *was* like Grandma and the other Madsen witches who'd come before.

"What is the rest?" I asked. "Just tell me, and I will say it."

"I can't," said Maeve. "The mirror won't let me. It's a doorway to the next world, and it's here to prevent spirits from crossing over."

"How did you get trapped?" I asked.

"It was Samhain, many years ago. I was angry with my mother, so I ran away. But then I found this mirror my mother had been working on, and when I looked into it, I spoke the same words you spoke. I didn't know that I would be stuck here forever. Or that my poor mother—"

"That your poor mother would die of grief. Just like Grandma said."

Maeve nodded sadly. "She looked for me all Samhain. She even checked the mirror but couldn't see me. It broke her heart, and she died. All she wanted was for us to be together. She didn't know it would end like this."

"I'm sorry," I said.

"There's more," said Maeve. A chill ran up my back.

"It's Samhain again. And you looked in the mirror and said the same words, Sly. If you don't find and speak the missing spell, you will get trapped in here too. Just like I did."

"No, that's not possible," I said. "I'm right here. I'm fine. See?" I patted my arms and legs. I was still here, on this side.

"You will begin to fade, like I did," said Maeve, "until you find yourself stuck over here with me."

"How do I stop it from happening?"

"My mother had a spell book. The missing words are in there. It's hidden somewhere on the grounds of the mansion. You must find it by midnight, Sly."

*Midnight!* I looked at the clock. Between sleeping in, eating waffles and now this, it was already noon! "But that's in exactly twelve hours! What if it's not enough time?"

"It's okay, Sly," she said. "I know where the book is."

"Then tell me!" I cried.

"I can't," she said. "The mirror won't let me. All I can do is give you clues. Riddles that will lead you to it."

My heart was pounding. "Riddles?"

"But we must move fast, Sly," said Maeve.

"What's this about riddles?" asked Grandma from behind me. "And what in Samhain is taking you so long to get ready?"

I spun around. "Grandma!"

"Oh, you opened that old thing," said Grandma. "I never could figure out the puzzle lock."

I stared at her. She obviously didn't see Maeve.

"What's that?" Grandma asked, looking at the mirror.

The first part of the spell appeared again, and before I could say anything, Grandma spoke the words. "Doras fosgailte."

"Stop!" I shouted.

But it was too late.

Grandma read the second line aloud. "Beatha ùr."

Grandma had cursed herself, and as I watched, she started to disappear!

“Grandma, no!” I screamed.

Grandma turned into a mist and then was gone. When I looked back in the mirror, there she was, standing next to Maeve.

“Grandma, are you okay?!”

“Oh dear,” she said. “That felt very strange. But yes, I am fine. I guess this must be the doorway Mildred Madsen made. It’s been under my nose for years!”

"I don't understand," I said. "Why did you go over there, but I'm still here?"

Grandma shrugged. "I'm old, Sly. And I spend a lot of time exploring the in-between. But don't you worry about me. I'll be fine."

She turned to Maeve and smiled. "Looks like I have a new friend."

"Hello," said Maeve. "I have been listening to you tell fortunes for years. It's nice to finally meet you. I'm Maeve."

"I know," said Grandma.

"I'm going to find the missing spell book," I said. "And I'm going to get you both out."

"I believe in you, Sly," said Grandma.

I looked at Maeve. "Let's do this. Tell me your riddles."

"I can only appear to you in mirrors," said Maeve. "I will do my best to follow you around as you search for clues."

I nodded. "Okay, I'm ready."

"Here is the first riddle," Maeve said.

For some reason I thought back to when I'd first arrived at Madsen Mansion. The great room. When I'd walked in, I'd noticed the echo.

"An echo!" I said. "The answer is an echo."

"Very good, Sly," said Grandma.

"I think I need to go to the great room."

"Hurry, Sly," said Maeve.

I ran down the spiral staircase, around and around, until I reached the great room.

"Echo!" I shouted, testing it out. Sure enough, my voice came back to me. *Echo... echo...*

I was in the right place, but what was I looking for?

Then I heard Grandma's voice coming from a speaking tube. "Trust your instincts," she said.

I looked for clues, searching high and low. But there was nothing. Then something, or rather someone, caught my eye.

It was the ghost girl, Maeve. But she wasn't in a mirror.

"I found you, Maeve," I said. "You're here in another painting."

"Yes, of course," said Grandma. "Her portrait is all over the mansion."

In this picture Maeve looked happier. She was smiling. And she was playing the piano.

"The piano," I said. "Could that be a clue?"

"Check the piano across the room," said Grandma.

I hurried over to the old piano and sat down at the bench. I didn't see anything unusual.

I heard Maeve's voice, more faintly now. "A riddle," she said.

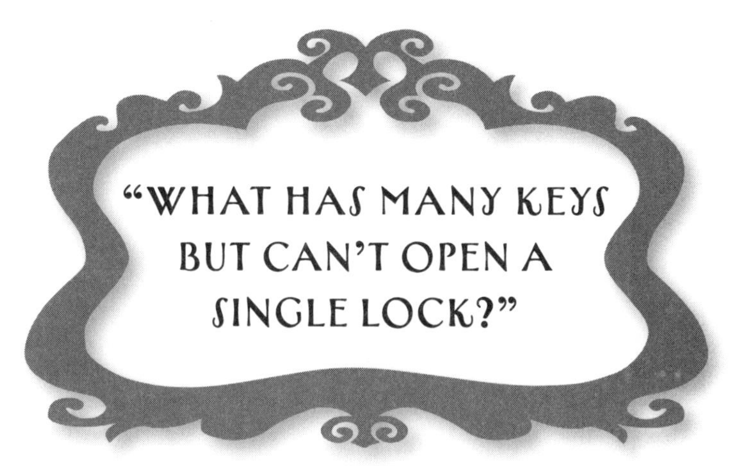


"Well, the answer is a piano, right?" I asked. "How does that help?" But Maeve was silent.

I stared at the piano. Keys, I thought. The keys!

I flipped open the lid and ran my hands over the keys. Everything seemed normal.

"Play something," said Grandma. Her voice sounded thin and far away too.

I could play a little bit. But what song?

"I know," I whispered. I played the first sad notes of Mom and Dad's favorite song. As I hit the fourth note, a flat, clunking sound came out. I hit the same key again. *Clu nk*.

"There's something wrong with this key." It was loose. I pulled on it, and it popped free.

Underneath was another key—a real key for a lock. But this one was an antique.

"Wow," I said. "It's a cool old key with an *M* on it."

"A skeleton key," said Grandma. "It will unlock anything in this house."

"If it opens everything, then how do I know what to unlock?"

"There must be something special," said Grandma. "Maeve?"

Maeve spoke.

Another riddle. I thought for a minute.

It must be an object with hands. But what?

"Is it a clock?" I asked at last.

"Of course! Very good, Sly," said Grandma.

I spun around and went to the grandfather clock. Just then it started to chime. *Bong, bong, bong, bong.*

"Oh no!" I cried. "It's already four o'clock? But how is that possible?"

"Time waits for no one," said Maeve.

"Don't worry, Sly," said Grandma. "Remember that time works differently in Madsen Mansion."

What clue did the clock hold? It was made of wood. It had a face and hands. All normal. But there in the cabinet was a keyhole. That had to be it!

I turned the key in the lock, and it opened.

"There's a paper inside," I said.

"What's on it?" asked Grandma, but I couldn't hear her very well.

I unfolded the paper. "It's a map," I said. "A map of Madsen Mansion."

I checked every spot on the map. There was the great room, my room in the tower, the kitchen, the grounds, even the dumbwaiter.

The dumbwaiter. I thought back to my trip up the little elevator. Then it dawned on me. This map wasn't complete after all. There was something missing.

"The mirror hallway," I said.

"What did you say?" asked Grandma. "You're so quiet, Sly. And I'm afraid the in-between is growing."

"The mirror hallway," I said more loudly. "It's not on this map."

"The thing that's missing may be as important as the thing that's there," said Grandma.

"I have to go there." I put the map in the inner pocket of my cape.

"Be careful, Sly," said Maeve. "Every time you look in a mirror, it will take more of your life from you. You could get trapped forever."

I didn't want to see that creepy hallway again, but I had to save Grandma and Maeve and keep myself from crossing over too.

I had to face my fear.

I ran to the kitchen. Who knew how long I had left? I couldn't trust time in this place.

I opened the dumbwaiter and climbed in, gathering my cape tighter, and used the pulley to haul myself up, up, up.

The dumbwaiter stopped, but I was only at the dining room. I had to go higher. I pulled the rope again until finally I reached the mirror hallway. I was scared to get out, but I forced myself to.

All around me, I saw myself reflected in mirrors. Over and over. Endless Slys, on and on forever. I tried to focus on just one

reflection, but I looked strange, like I was fuzzy around the edges.

Grandma and Maeve appeared in the mirror beside me. Their reflections were so faint!

"Grandma," I said. "You're fading, and I think I'm fading too."

"You must hurry, Sly," she said.

"The next riddle," said Maeve.

"That's easy," I said. "It's a mirror. But I'm here already. What more is there?"

"Maybe it's about *what* you see," said Grandma. "Maybe you have to pick the right mirror."

Which one? *Make two people out of one.* I moved around the hall, looking in all the mirrors until one of them showed two of me side by side. This had to be the right one.

"What do I do?" I asked. "Do I try to open it somehow?"

I reached out to put my hand on the mirror, but it just kept going.

"What's happening?" I cried.

"Don't worry, Sly," said Grandma. "I think it's an illusion. The mirrors are hiding an empty space. There's no glass there."

I leaned in farther and discovered it was just an empty frame with another mirror set back a few feet behind it. I stepped through the frame and into another little hallway.

"It's a secret passageway!"

It opened into a dark room. There was a small table with a candle in a fancy holder and a box of matches. There was also a bookshelf.

I struck a match and lit the candle, then placed the box of matches in my cape pocket with the map.

"The table has a riddle carved into it," I said.

# "WHAT HAS WORDS BUT NEVER SPEAKS?"

I carried the candle around the room, looking for clues. *Words, words, words.* I stopped at the bookshelf. *Books have words, but they don't speak.*

The answer had to be a book! Could one of these be the spell book I was looking for?

I checked the spines of the books. Nothing stood out to me, so I pulled out the books one by one and flipped through them. There were no notes or spells or keys—no clues at all.

The last book on the shelf was blue and gold. I pulled it out and saw an *M* on the cover. My heart raced. *Yes! This must be it!* I opened it and flipped through the pages, but they were blank. No spells. Nothing. Then finally, on the very last page, there was a riddle written in tiny letters.

I read it out loud.

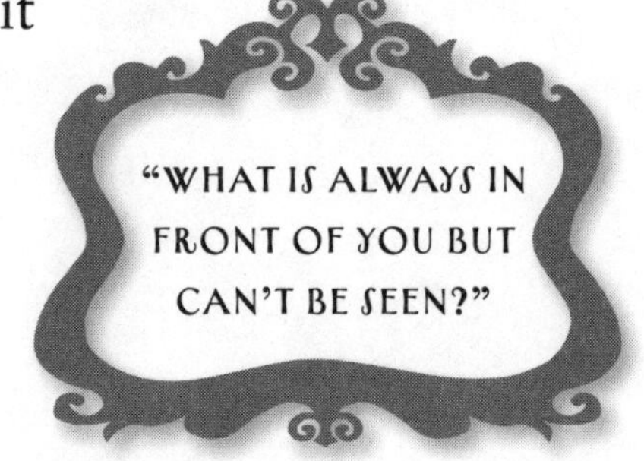

My mind was blank. And I was so tired. I had no idea what time it was, but it felt late. Unnaturally late. How long had I been in the little room?

I didn't feel right. I held my hand in front of my face, and it looked blurry. I was fading!

In a panic I ran back to the mirror hallway, but when I saw my reflection again, I was even more scared. I was so hard to see! And Grandma and Maeve were nothing but wisps in the mirror. I was losing them—and losing myself!

"We're all disappearing!" I cried.

"The mirrors are taking your energy," said Grandma. "Get away to give yourself more time!"

"It's too late for us," called Maeve. "Go, and don't look back."

"Save yourself!" urged Grandma. "I will always be with you."

"I will find a way," I shouted. "Don't disappear!"

I dove for the little elevator, used the pulley to race down to the kitchen and arrived with a *thud*. But getting away didn't help me feel any more solid. I had to solve this tough riddle—and soon. But I couldn't figure it out. If only I could have some help. If only I could talk to Mom and Dad.

That's it! I thought, as I spied the old phone on the kitchen wall.

I lifted the earpiece. Now to call Mom. How did this thing work again? We'd had a rotary phone at home for decoration, but Mom had shown me how to use it. *Okay, first number*. I put my finger in the numbered hole and pulled the dial. I continued with the rest of Mom's phone number, watching the dial spin around. *Click, click, click*. It was so *slow*.

Mom answered on the first ring. "Sly?" she said. "Is everything okay?

"Hi," I said. There was a big lump in my throat.

"It's late, honey. It's past ten o'clock. I thought you'd be asleep by now."

"It is?" I asked. So much time had gone by! "I needed to hear your voice."

"Oh, honey," said Mom. "I was just talking to Dad. Why don't I put you both on speaker so we can all talk?"

The lump in my throat got a little smaller. "That sounds good."

"Hi, buddy," said Dad. His voice sounded far away. "Why are you still up?"

I thought for a moment. I didn't want to scare them, and I didn't have time to tell the whole story. "I was thinking of a riddle, and I couldn't fall asleep without solving it."

"Oh, riddles. I love riddles," said Dad. "Hit me."

"What is always in front of you but can't be seen?" I said.

"Hmm," said Mom. "That's a thinker."

There was a long moment of silence.

"I think I've got it," said Dad. "It's the future. It's always in front of you even if you can't see it."

"Of course," I said. "That's it!" But what did it mean?

"Can you go to sleep now, Sly? Or is something else worrying you?" asked Mom.

"No, I'm fine," I said. "I guess I miss you guys. Both of you. And..."

"What is it, buddy" asked Dad.

"If I come home—I mean, *when* I come home—I don't want to choose between you. I want to be with you both. I don't want to see you just *sometimes*, Dad."

There was silence on the other end. Then Dad spoke. "We've been talking, Sly, and we think that's best too. I'm working on a way to live closer to you."

"But no matter where we are, we are always going to be a family unit," said Mom. "Dad and I will figure it out. We're a team."

"I love you guys," I said. "But I've gotta go." I had to save Grandma and Maeve.

I hung up before they could say anything else. The future, I thought. But what did it mean? It was in front of me, but I couldn't *see* it? Where was the future? Where, where, where? How could I find it? If only I had a map of the future, I thought. Everything would be easier then. *Wait*. A map of the future? The map!

I pulled the old map from my pocket. Maybe I had missed something before? I scanned the rooms of the house. Nothing out of the ordinary. One of the outbuildings? The old stables? The shed? Wait a minute—the Madsen graveyard! There on the map, in the middle of the cemetery, was a tiny building. A tomb. And on it was a symbol. The Bowen knot.

I stood outside the kitchen door and stared at the empty pie dish. *Something* had eaten the pie. Frantically I scanned the grounds of Madness Mansion for anything that looked like it wanted to eat me. The grounds were clear all the way to the cemetery. I shuddered. The trees were creepy enough during the day, but now that it was dark, they were terrifying! Who knew what was hiding behind them? And I had to go to the cemetery? On Samhain? I gulped.

It was now or never, I took off running. I figured the faster I went, the better. No time to think about the bats flying overhead. No time to think about the menacing mist rolling across the ground.

The moon was high in the sky. Too high. Time was speeding by. Soon it would be midnight. I ran faster, trying to outrun the night and the feeling that something was chasing me. I looked over my shoulder, expecting spirits to grab me at any moment, but there was nothing there. When I turned back around, I ran right into the outstretched claws of a monster with wings and pointed teeth. "No!" I screamed as I fell back onto the cold ground. "Get away!" I kicked and thrashed as my cape swirled around me and covered my face. Finally I gave up and waited for whatever it was to eat me. But all was quiet.

Slowly I peeked out. The moon shone down on a large statue. It wasn't a monster after all—at least, not a real one. It was the entrance to the graveyard.

I stood up and walked through the gateway on shaking legs. The little graveyard was filled with broken headstones and statues that were missing arms and legs. With each step, I expected something to reach out and grab me. I forced myself to stay strong and continue, and finally I found what I was looking for.

Nestled at the base of a twisted tree was a little stone building with steps leading down into it. And on the door was the Bowen knot.

All I had to do was go in. Just go in and find the spell book. Just go in and undo the curse that held Maeve and Grandma and me. Just go in and save us all. But I didn't feel like I had the strength. I was so tired. It was so late. I was all alone. And I was running out of time.

I took a deep breath and thought of Mom and Dad. I had to believe in myself if I was ever going to see them again. I had to try.

With a shaking hand I pushed on the Bowen knot, and the door groaned open. A gust of cold, musty air blew out.

I swallowed a scream and stepped inside.

It was dark and damp, lit only by the moonlight that shone through the iron-barred windows. The tomb was empty, save for a single candle on top of a long stone box with an *M* carved on it.

"A coffin," I whispered. I was alone in a tomb with a coffin. In the dark.

I fumbled in my cape for the box of matches. I lit one, but it went out. *Come on.*

I tried two more before I was finally able to light the candle. *Whew*.

I held it up, and the flame flared. The light glowed inside the small room, illuminating the name on the coffin—Mildred Madsen. Maeve's mother.

There were more words etched on the end of the coffin. Another riddle.

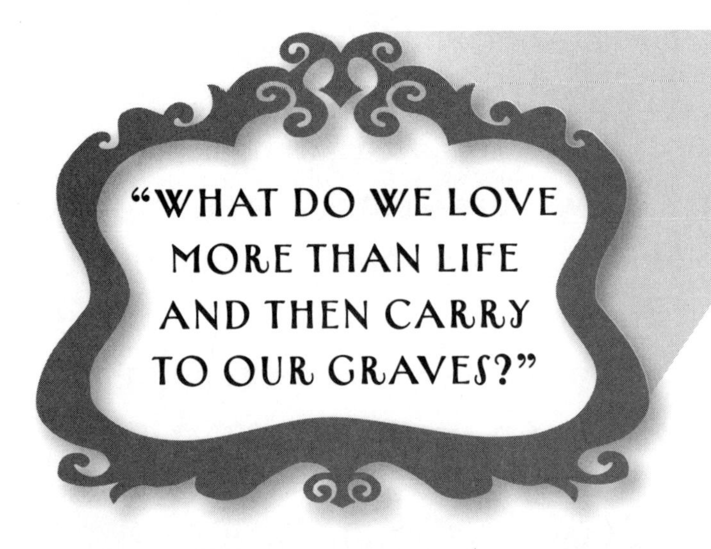


What did I love more than life? Besides my family? Nothing, I guessed. *Wait*. Was

that the answer? Yes. The answer was "nothing."

I stared at the coffin. Did Mildred Madsen carry nothing to her grave too? Or was this a way of telling me that she *did* carry something? And maybe that something was in the coffin.

"No," I said, backing away. "That's too much. I can't do it."

I felt woozy and nearly fell over. I looked down at my hands. I could almost see right through them. It was happening. I was disappearing!

"Come on, Sly," I said aloud to myself. "Finish this."

I set the candle down and struggled to move the coffin lid. It was so heavy. I pushed with everything I had, and it slid to the side.

With a trembling hand I raised the candle. Was there a skeleton in there?

I peeked in and saw a small bundle wrapped in cloth. No bones, no scary ghosts, nothing else at all.

I picked up the bundle and unwrapped it. It was a book with the Bowen knot on its cover.

I flipped through the pages. It was filled with handwriting in Gaelic and what looked like recipes for strange concoctions. There was a drawing of the mirror cabinet. This had to be the spell book. I had found it at last!

"Finally!" I shouted and accidentally blew out the candle.

I had to hurry. I ran from the tomb, across the grounds and back into the kitchen.

The clock in the great hall started to chime. *Bong!*

I looked at the clock on the stove. It said *11:59*. One minute to midnight. *Oh no!* I had to speak the spell into the mirror before the clock struck twelve!

I sprinted down the hall. *Bong!*

Up the tower stairs. *Bong!*

Around and around. *Bong!*

Up, up, up. My legs wobbled. *Bong!*

I burst into the hexagon room. *Bong!*

Ran to the cabinet. *Bong!*

Maeve and Grandma were in the mirror, but they were almost invisible. *Bong!*

I was fading fast. It felt like I was wading through pudding. *Bong!*

"Hurry, Sly," Grandma called, her voice thin and weak. *Bong!*

I fumbled with the pages of the spell book. Where was it? *Bong!*

Just as I thought all was lost, I turned to the page with the drawing of the mirror cabinet. Below it was a spell. The first two phrases I recognized. But the last one was new. I screamed it out.

"Thig air ais thugam!"

*Bong!*

The clock struck midnight, and I fell to the floor.

Darkness washed over me.

*Come back to me.*

A voice in the darkness. I blinked as I came to, trying to see who it was.

"Grandma!" I threw myself into her arms. "You're here."

"I am," she said.

"Where are we? Are we in the mirror or out?" I asked.

"Look," she said. She pointed to the room, the bed, my backpack. "You brought us back. You spoke the final words of the spell. 'Thig air ais thugam.'"

"What does it mean?" I asked.

"Come back to me."

I'd done it. I'd saved Grandma from the mirror. I'd saved myself from becoming a ghost kid forever. But where was Maeve?

"Maeve!" I called out.

"I'm here, Sly," she said. She floated from the shadows, gliding across the room in her white nightgown. She was still pale, but she didn't look sad anymore.

"I'm so glad you're free," I said.

"Thanks to you, Sly." Maeve smiled. "I will always remember you."

"Wait, what do you mean?" I asked. "Where are you going?"

She started to fade away. "It's not my time anymore," she said.

"But we've only just met."

"You're the one who saw me. The one who listened," said Maeve. "Now I can finally rest."

With that she turned into mist and was gone.

"Goodbye," I whispered. "I'll never forget you either."

It took me a long time to settle down, so Grandma and I snuggled up by the fireplace and snoozed on the couch, my cape wrapped tightly around me. Morning came fast, and we were both starving, so we went straight to eating waffles. Grandma even put ice cream on them this time!

"Can't wait to go home, I bet," said Grandma.

I shook my head. "No way. I love it here. With you."

Grandma smiled. "You will be back," she said. "There are definitely more mysteries within the walls of Madsen Mansion." She winked.

What else could Madness Mansion throw at me? "Bring it on," I said with a grin.

When Mom came to pick me up, I felt ready to see our new place. I wasn't sure what it would be like, but I knew it would be okay. And I knew Mom and Dad would make sure our family stayed a family—wherever we were.

As we drove away, I looked back at Madsen Mansion. I saw a faint glow coming from the tower. What was that? Before now, I would have thought it was just sunlight glinting off the window. But now I knew that anything was possible, because Madsen Mansion was no ordinary house—and I was no ordinary kid. I came from a long line of powerful Madsen witches, after all.

I reached into my cape pocket and touched my Bowen-knot charm. When I needed it again, I would be ready. For anything.

## AUTHOR ACKNOWLEDGMENTS

Thank you to everyone at the Orca Pod for your hard work and dedication, and for the opportunity to write my very first illustrated book for younger readers. I feel incredibly lucky to have artwork by Alyssa Waterbury on these pages. Thank you, Alyssa, for so thoroughly capturing the story and for bringing my characters to life. I can't wait for kids to discover your drawings. Thank you to editor Debbie Rogosin for your careful eye. You asked all the right questions to make this little book of my heart come alive. Huge thanks to my wonderful agent, Stacey Kondla, for your guidance and enthusiasm. I am forever grateful to Tanya Trafford for opening the door to this book and for championing my strange ideas. Thank you to my kids and your love of stories. This book is for those who live in the in-between places, as all the very best people do.

CREDIT: LAURA HOUSDEN

**BROOKE CARTER** is a Canadian novelist and the author of several contemporary books for teens, including *Double or Nothing* (Junior Library Guild Gold Selection), *Learning Seventeen* (CCBC Best Book for Teens) and *Sulfur Heart* from the Orca Soundings line. She earned her MFA in creative writing at UBC.

CREDIT: JILL WATERBURY

**ALYSSA WATERBURY** is an illustrator from London, Ontario. A graduate of the Sheridan College illustration program, her work aims to keep things thoughtful, with a dash of playfulness.